FIX IT, Sam

Lori Ries

Illustrated by Sue Ramá

ini Charlesbridge

Sam can
fix anything.

Uh-oh.

Sam, help?
Fix the toys?

Thanks, Sam!

Uh-oh. Sam, help?
Fix the pillow?

Way to go, Sam!

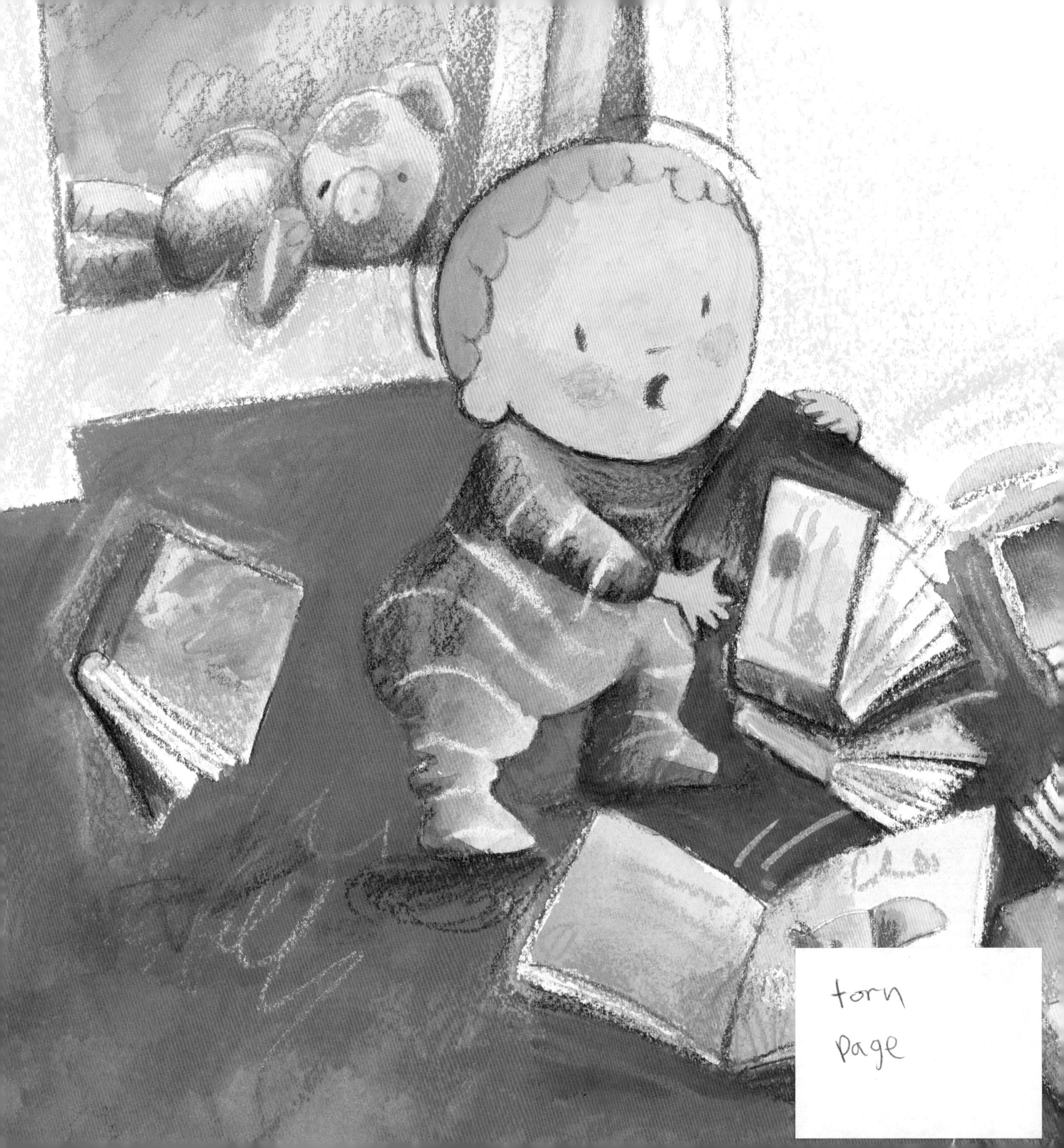

Uh-oh. Sam, help?
Fix the books?

Thanks again, Sam!

Uh-oh. Sam, help?
Fix the blanket?

Hooray for Sam!

Uh-oh. Sam, help?

Look
what
I made!

Uh-oh.
Who can
fix this?

I can fix anything!

For Daniel, Katie, Jennifer—and David, with love. Thanks for all the giggles and tent play.
And for Mr. Joe Anderson, who told me that if I worked hard enough,
I could become a great writer. Thank you for being a caring teacher.
I wish you the best as you leave Helena High School.
—L. R.

To Sherry Lynn Lulu, my very own Fix-it Sister.
—S. R.

Text copyright © 2007 by Lori Ries
Illustrations copyright © 2007 by Sue Ramá
All rights reserved, including the right of
reproduction in whole or in part in any form.
Charlesbridge and colophon are registered
trademarks of Charlesbridge Publishing, Inc.

Published by Charlesbridge
85 Main Street
Watertown, MA 02472
(617) 926-0329
www.charlesbridge.com

Illustrations done in colored pencil, water-soluble
  crayon, and watercolor
Display and text type set in Lemonade
Color separations by Chroma Graphics, Singapore
Printed and bound by Regent Publishing Services
Production supervision by Brian G. Walker
Designed by Diane M. Earley

Library of Congress Cataloging-in-Publication Data
Ries, Lori.
  Fix it, Sam / Lori Ries ; illustrated by Sue Ramá.
    p. cm.
  Summary: Sam is good at fixing things, but his
little brother Petey is the one who keeps their tent
from falling.
  ISBN 978-1-57091-598-7 (reinforced for library use)
  ISBN 978-1-57091-722-6 (softcover)
  [1. Brothers—Fiction.] I. Ramá, Sue, ill. II. Title.
PZ7.R429Fix 2007
[E]—dc22   2006009028

Printed in China
(hc) 10 9 8 7 6 5 4 3 2 1
(sc) 10 9 8 7 6 5 4 3 2 1